D1123317

A DOG'S LIFE

BY
CAROLINE
SHERMAN

ILLUSTRATED BY
DONALD
WU

Amazon Children's Publishing

For Martin, of course

—C.S.

To Chip the Wonderdog!

—D.W.

Amazon Publishing
Attn: Amazon Children's Books
P.O. Box 400818
Las Vegas, NV 89149
www.amazon.com/amazonchildrenspublishing

Library of Congress Cataloging-in-Publication Data

Sherman, Caroline.
A dog's life / by Caroline Sherman ; illustrated by Donald Wu. — 1st ed.
p. cm.
Summary: A pet dog demonstrates why the popular belief that dogs lead an easy life is completely false.
ISBN 978-0-7614-6200-2 (hardcover) — ISBN 978-0-7614-6201-9 (ebook)
[1. Dogs--Fiction. 2. Humorous stories.] I. Wu, Donald, ill. II. Title.
PZ7.S54524Do 2012
[E]—dc23
2011048165

The illustrations are rendered digitally.
Book design by Anahid Hamparian
Editor: Margery Cuyler

Printed in China (W)
First edition
10 9 8 7 6 5 4 3 2 1
Amazon Children's Publishing

EVERYONE THINKS THAT DOGS HAVE IT EASY.
But I work from morning till night.

As soon as I get up . . .

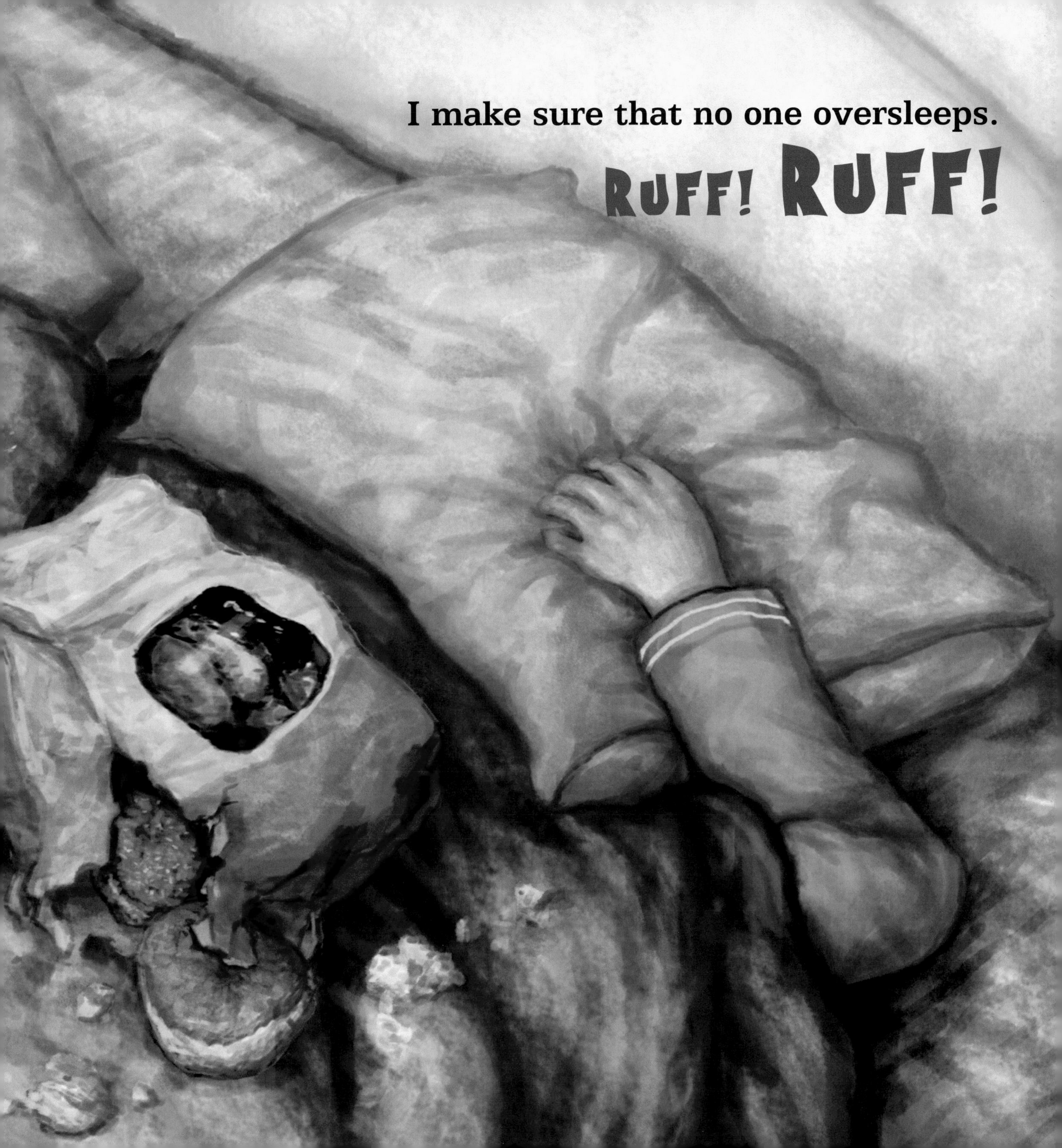

I make sure that no one oversleeps.

RUFF! RUFF!

Then I go outside to tidy up the yard.

SPLISH! SPLASH!

I sweep the floor. **SWISH! SWISH!**

I answer every doorbell and make guests feel at home.

WOOF! WOOF!

I always fetch the balls that humans like to throw.

I wash dishes.

SLURP! SLURP!

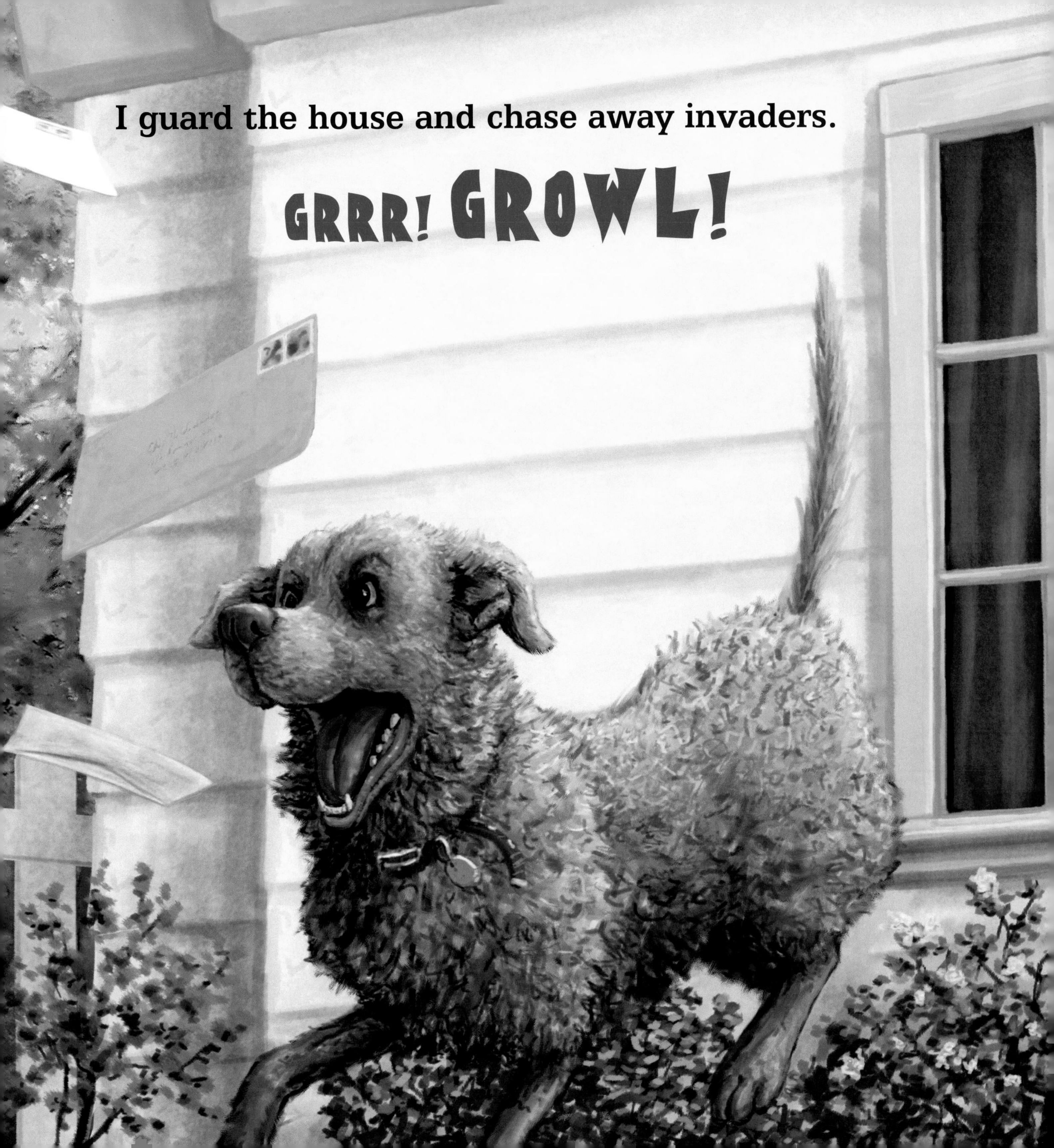

I guard the house and chase away invaders.

GRRR! GROWL!

I inspect the trash for anything I can recycle.

MUNCH! MUNCH!

MILK
Low Fat

I keep the humans warm,
since they don't have any fur.

Zzzz . . .

And at night, I sing lullabies until everyone is asleep.

I don't know how they'd manage without me!